MR. TICKLE
and the Scary Halloween

originated by Roger Hargreaves

Written and illustrated by Adam Hargreaves

PSS!
PRICE STERN SLOAN
An Imprint of Penguin Group (USA) LLC

There was a time, Mr. Tickle thought to himself, when Halloween was fun.

But not anymore.

Not since Little Miss Scary had moved to town.

Now, Halloween was downright scary.

Scare-your-pants-off scary.

Last year, Little Miss Scary had scared the smile off Mr. Happy.

She had scared the bows off Little Miss Giggles.

And she even had scared the hat off Mr. Brave!

Little Miss Scary had scared everyone.

"But this year will be different!" Mr. Tickle said to himself.

Little Miss Scary was very excited about Halloween this year.

She had everything ready. As she left her house to go trick-or-treating, she couldn't help chuckling to herself.

Oh, what fun she was going to have!

Her first victim was Little Miss Ditzy.

And the plan for Little Miss Ditzy was to creep up behind her and drop a huge plastic spider on her head.

But as she sneaked up on Little Miss Ditzy, there was something sneaking up behind Little Miss Scary.

An extraordinarily long thing.

A thing that tickled her.

Little Miss Scary burst out laughing.

And as you most probably know, it is very difficult
to be scary when you are laughing.

"Hello, Little Miss Scary," said Little Miss Ditzy. "I like
your spider. Are you going to a Halloween party?"

Little Miss Scary was annoyed that her scary trick hadn't
worked. She stomped off without saying a word.

Little Miss Scary's next trick was to paint herself with glow-in-the-dark paint and swing on a rope from the branch of a tree.

But as she sat on the branch waiting for Mr. Bump to come by, that extraordinarily long something reached up into the tree and tickled her again.

She laughed so much that she fell right out of the tree!

Shortly afterward, Mr. Bump found her swinging upside down.

"Hello, Little Miss Scary," said Mr. Bump, laughing. "That looks like the kind of thing that happens to me!"

Little Miss Scary could only scowl.

Every time Little Miss Scary tried to scare someone, something would tickle her.

Now, we all know who that was, don't we? But Little Miss Scary could not figure it out.

It was turning out to be a very frustrating Halloween.

And so it went on all night.

She had planned to cover Little Miss Neat in green goo, but she laughed so much she spilled it on herself.

She was going to scare Mr. Quiet by creeping up behind him and banging two trash-can lids together, but she laughed so much she fell in one of the cans and got stuck.

And she was going to scare Mr. Grumpy with
a rubber bat, but she was laughing so much even
Mr. Grumpy thought it was funny!

On her way home, Little Miss Scary met Mr. Tickle.

"How was your Halloween?" asked Mr. Tickle.

"Not much fun," replied Little Miss Scary, gloomily.
"Not so much trick-or-treating as . . ."

"Tickle-treating?" suggested Mr. Tickle.

And he laughed so hard that tears rolled down his face.